Chicken or Egg

For Cameron: You. Me. Hockey. Whoopee! —BSM

For Christopher, who always chooses "we"—SDS

Published by
MAGINATION PRESS®
An Educational Publishing Foundation Book
American Psychological Association
750 First Street NE
Washington, DC 20002

Magination Press is a registered trademark of the American Psychological Association.

For more information about our books, including a complete catalog, please write to us, call 1-800-374-2721, or visit our website at www.apa.org/pubs/magination.

Book design by Gwen Grafft
Printed by Lake Book Manufacturing Inc., Melrose Park, IL

Library of Congress Cataloging-in-Publication Data
Names: Miles, Brenda, author. | Sweet, Susan D., author. | Melon + Mandarina.
Title: Chicken or Egg : who comes first? / by Brenda S. Miles, PhD, and Susan
    D. Sweet, PhD ; Illustrated by Melon + Mandarina.
Description: Washington, DC : Magination Press, American Psychological
    Association, [2017] | Summary: Chicken and Egg compete in sports, on
    tests, and in other ways until they discover that winning and losing are
    less fun than playing together.
Identifiers: LCCN 2016050780 | ISBN 9781433827198 (hardcover) |
    ISBN 1433827190 (hardcover)
Subjects: | CYAC: Winning and losing—Fiction. | Competition
    (Psychology)—Fiction. | Chickens—Fiction. | Eggs—Fiction.
Classification: LCC PZ8.3.M5762 Chi 2017 | DDC [E]—dc23 LC record available
at https://lccn.loc.gov/2016050780

Manufactured in the United States of America
10 9 8 7 6 5 4 3 2 1

Chicken or Egg

Who Comes First?

By Brenda S. Miles, PhD,
and Susan D. Sweet, PhD

Illustrated by Melon + Mandarina

Magination Press • Washington, DC • American Psychological Association

Chicken or Egg.
Who comes first?

Run. Won! No fun.

Hill. Thrill! Spill.

Fast. Passed! Last.

Roll. Hole. Goal!

Ball. Tall! Too small.

Test. Best! Not impressed.

Fly! Try... Why?

You won. All done.

Nothing to do. Feeling blue.
No me and you.

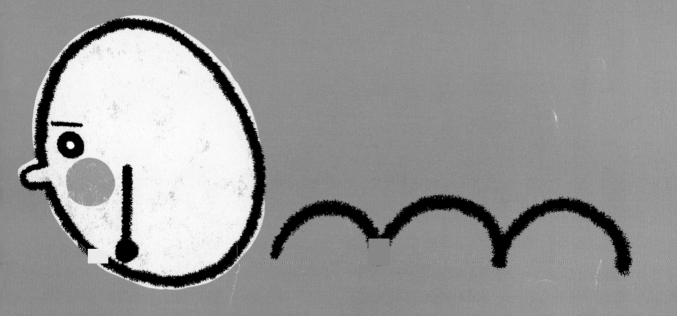

Lost. Found! Stick around.
One. Two.
Much more we can do!

Home run. You won. *Still* fun!

Chase. Last place. Great race!

Chicken and Egg.
You. Me. We.
Whoopee!

Note to Parents & Other Caregivers

You've probably heard the age-old question, "Which came first—the chicken or the egg?" The answer is certainly debatable. Maybe it was the chicken, or maybe the egg, or maybe the answer isn't clear. When it comes to being first, though, one thing is clear: Being number one can feel great, and it's something many of us—okay, maybe all of us—want, whether competing on the playground or vying for the corner office.

Hopefully you've enjoyed some great successes in your life. Maybe you were the last one out in a game of tag, or first in your graduating class. Victory is sweet. But for every win, there was probably a loss—maybe many of them! And while none of us enjoy losing, all of us have to learn to deal with it. It's an inevitable part of life. Why? Because there will always be someone out there who is better than we are at just about everything, no matter how hard we try. But knowing we can't always come first shouldn't mean we steer clear of challenge or competition. After all, while giving up may protect us from defeat, it also means we miss out on valuable opportunities to learn and do better the next time. Many highly successful people credit their failures with ultimately helping them reach their goals. Their failures were a necessary step on the path to achievement.

Losing gracefully and persisting through failure are great lessons to learn, especially while we are young. It can help with everything from making and keeping friends to building a fulfilling career. And here's the good news! You can help your child learn to accept disappointments, bounce back, and try again. These skills are part of being resilient. Resilience helps us cope with stress and manage disappointment. It's an important life skill, and a huge predictor of success.

Competition in Context

We all feel some degree of competitiveness. It's part of being human (or a chicken…or an egg!). And while competing for food may not be as critical now as it was before the advent of grocery stores, modern-day sporting events are big business—proof positive that our competitive spirit is thriving. Children feel competitive, too, although natural variations mean some children feel more competitive than others. That competitiveness may also appear with some playmates more than others, and siblings usually top the list!

Competitiveness itself is not a bad thing, but extreme negative reactions to loss can be disruptive and upsetting when everyone is trying to have fun. Children in particular may find losing tough. Part of the reason involves their brains, which continue to grow and develop until early adulthood. Until their brains are fully mature, children don't think about and process information the way we do as adults. For one thing, they often engage in "all-or-none" thinking, which is more concrete or black and white than adult thought. So there are winners *or* losers, there is first *or* last, and there is good *or* bad with little understanding of any middle ground or more abstract concepts like luck. Children sometimes struggle to understand other people's viewpoints, too, so they may not appreciate how a victor might feel about a tantrum displayed by an opponent. Children may also lack the vocabulary to fully express frustration, so disappointment may surface as anger or tears instead.

Learning to lose gracefully takes some time. But with support and practice, children can and do get better at it! Here are some strategies to help you get started.

Focus on Effort, Not Outcome

If you focus on winning versus effort, then losing can really hurt, at any age. Don't make winning everything, and resist the urge to compare your child with siblings, classmates, or highly skilled students and athletes in the neighborhood. To stoke the competitive spirit, focus on fun as well as personal accomplishments. For example, asking, "Did you play your best?," "Did you beat your own record?" or "Did you have fun?"

is more supportive and helpful for building resilience than "Did you win?" It's okay to share disappointment with your child when losing happens. Losing is hard for everyone. But don't get stuck there. Move on to something that shifts the focus, like praising your child for great effort throughout the game. When Chicken and Egg shift the focus from winning to fun, they both feel better.

Practice Losing

It takes practice to win, but it takes practice to lose, too. As tempting as it might be to let your child win when you play together, resist the urge to let them win every time. Your home provides a safe and supportive setting to practice both winning and losing. As you play together, practice a variety of skills like turn-taking, following the rules, and playing fair. Be sure to play cooperative games now and then, too, where you work together to accomplish a goal. Cooperation is a big part of fun and fair play.

Set the Stage

When our adrenaline is pumping we tend to be impulsive, and act before thinking. Our bodies are designed that way so we can escape danger the instant it appears. But the adrenaline that surges when we're in danger is the same adrenaline that pumps when we're excited in a big game—so acting without thinking can happen then, too. Have a brief discussion with your child at the beginning of a game or competition, before excitement swells. Talk about being a good sport and having fun. Adrenaline will still run high, but setting the stage may help guide your child in the moment, especially if you deliver the message often.

Instruct With Specifics

It's great to tell your child to "play fair" or be "a good sport" but young brains that think concretely don't necessarily know what those terms mean. Be specific and explain what being a good sport is all about. For example, it means not bragging when you win, and congratulating your opponent when you lose. As Egg learned, playing and losing are still more fun than storming off and not playing at all.

Model

Children model what they see. Whether you are playing yourself or watching your child play, consider your language and show respect. Be generous with praise for all players. Clap when either team scores. Shake hands with opponents, win or lose. When cheering for your child, are you proud that they studied, prepared, played hard, and supported their team? Or is the scoreboard or test grade clearly more important to you? Watch your words and tone and what they may communicate. Make sure other adults in your child's life are positive role models, too, focusing on effort, growth, improvement, and conduct rather than winning or losing.

Find Other Examples

Chicken and Egg experience winning and losing across many situations. Additional examples are everywhere. Watch sports with your child and discuss players who are winning or losing. Are they reacting poorly or gracefully? Point out resilience when you see it. Did a player miss a basket but keep trying to score throughout the game? Did someone lose a singing competition but still sing with joy? Talk about the importance of bouncing back from disappointment and never giving up.

Point Out the Good Stuff

If your child handles a win well, point it out. The same goes for a loss. Focus on things your child did well, win or lose, and be specific in your compliments. Did your child play with determination or show improvement in a specific skill? Did your child stay motivated even when behind? Did your child cheer on friends and classmates? It's always great to hear about the good stuff, and knowing what we did well can shape our behavior in positive ways.

Learn From Losses

There are important lessons to be learned from losing, but focus on improving rather than winning if your child shows a desire to do better next time. Maybe your child was tired, hit a streak of bad luck, or the team was clearly outplayed. Maybe there's a skill your child could practice, or a playbook your child could study. It is fine to talk about improving for next time, but focus on fun and skill-building rather than winning at any cost. Even the best athletes lose sometimes; it's all part of the game and what keeps us coming back for more! The important thing is to show up and keep trying, no matter what—in sports, other types of competition, and life. As hockey great Wayne Gretzky once said, "You miss 100% of the shots you don't take." And that's an important lesson, win or lose.

Seek Support

If your child struggles with losing, whether in sports, the arts, academics, or otherwise, talk to your child's coach, trainer, or teacher about the triggers for frustration. Then brainstorm strategies that might be supportive. If your child's struggles seem more extreme or concerning, seek the support of a licensed professional such as a pediatrician, child psychologist, or child psychiatrist.

About the Authors

Brenda S. Miles, PhD, is a pediatric neuropsychologist who has worked in hospital, rehabilitation, and school settings. She is an author and co-author of several books for children, including *Move Your Mood!* and *Stickley Sticks to It!: A Frog's Guide to Getting Things Done.* Brenda encourages children and adults to make time for play—each and every day!

Susan D. Sweet, PhD, is a clinical child psychologist and mother of two. She has worked in hospital, school, and community-based settings and is passionate about children's mental health and well-being. Susan hopes all children find the fun in play—no matter who comes first!

Susan and Brenda have also co-authored *Princess Penelopea Hates Peas: A Tale of Picky Eating and Avoiding Catastropeas* and *King Calm: Mindful Gorilla in the City.*

About the Illustrator

Melon + Mandarina has been working in the illustration field for almost 10 years now. She grew up in Peru and studied painting at the Fine Arts School of Lima. As an artist, she works with a variety of media including pencil, ink, watercolor, and digital media. She feels that illustration is a wonderful way to express herself while working with the creative tools she loves. Melon + Mandarina works and lives in Peru.

About Magination Press

Magination Press is an imprint of the American Psychological Association, the largest scientific and professional organization representing psychologists in the United States and the largest association of psychologists worldwide.